L l

leopard
lion

Mm

man
monkey
mule

Nn

nurse

Oo

ostrich
otter

P p

pelican
pier
pig

Qq

queen

R r

rabbit
raven
robot
rose

Ss

sea
seal
sun

Tt

tigers
train
turkey

Uu

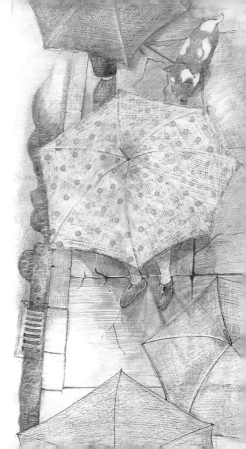

umbrellas

V v

violin
volcano
vulture

Ww

wasp
weasel
wedding
wolf

X x

xylophone

Yy

yak

Z z

zebras
zoo

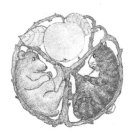

Aladdin Books

Macmillan Publishing Company

866 Third Avenue, New York, NY 10022

Maxwell Macmillan Canada, Inc.

First Aladdin Books edition 1993

Copyright © 1971 by Helen Oxenbury

First published 1971

Miniature edition first published 1992 by

William Heinemann Ltd.

Michelin House

81 Fulham Road

London SW3 6RB

From an original layout and design by Jan Pienkowski

1 2 3 4 5 6 7 8 9 10

ISBN 0-689-71761-X

Printed and bound in the UK by BPCC Hazells Ltd.

Member of BPCC Ltd.